MW00886597

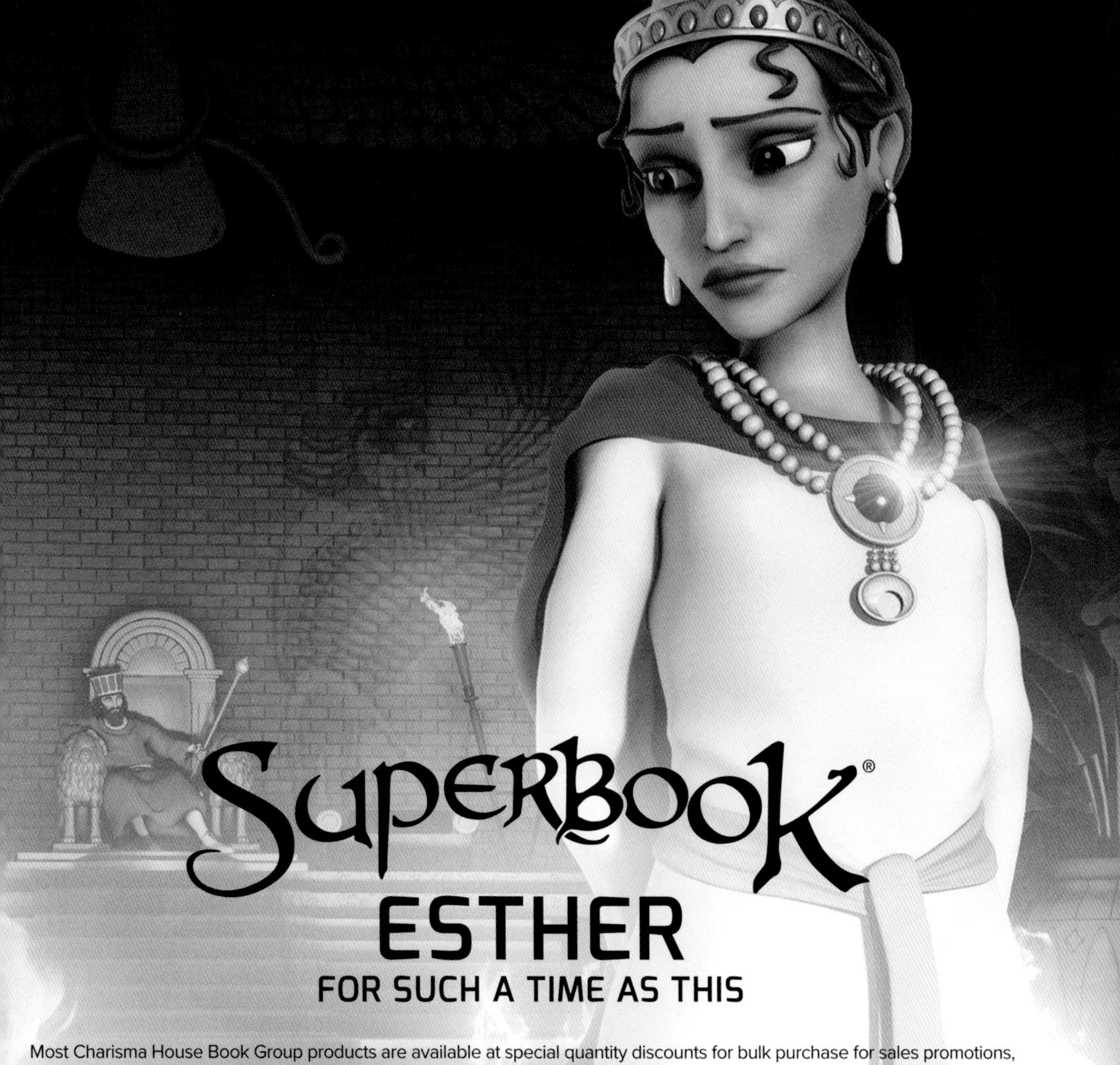

ESTHER

FOR SUCH A TIME AS THIS

Most Charisma House Book Group products are available at special quantity discounts for bulk purchase for sales promotions, premiums, fund-raising, and educational needs. For details, call us at (407) 333-0600 or visit our website at charismahouse.com.

Story adapted by Gwen Ellis et al. and published by Charisma House, 600 Rinehart Road, Lake Mary, Florida 32746

International Standard Book Number: 978-1-62999-845-9

20 21 22 23 24 — 987654321

Printed in China

School was about to begin when Joy saw a girl in a wheelchair looking a little lost.

“Hi, I’m Joy,” she said. “Need some help?”

“Yes, please!” the girl replied. “My name is Bonnie Scott. I’m looking for room 12, but my GPS is not working in this new school.”

“Oh, I’ll walk you there,” said Joy with a smile. The two girls quickly became friends as they went down the hall together.

As Bonnie went into her class, Joy saw Janice, the president of the girls' club.

"Janice, I know the person I'll choose to be a new member of our club!" Joy said happily.

"You mean that girl in the wheelchair?" Janice frowned. "She's not right for our club. She can't decorate the school or cheer at games or anything."

"Sure she can," Joy said.

"Well, I think choosing her would be a bad idea for you, Joy." Then Janice walked away without saying goodbye.

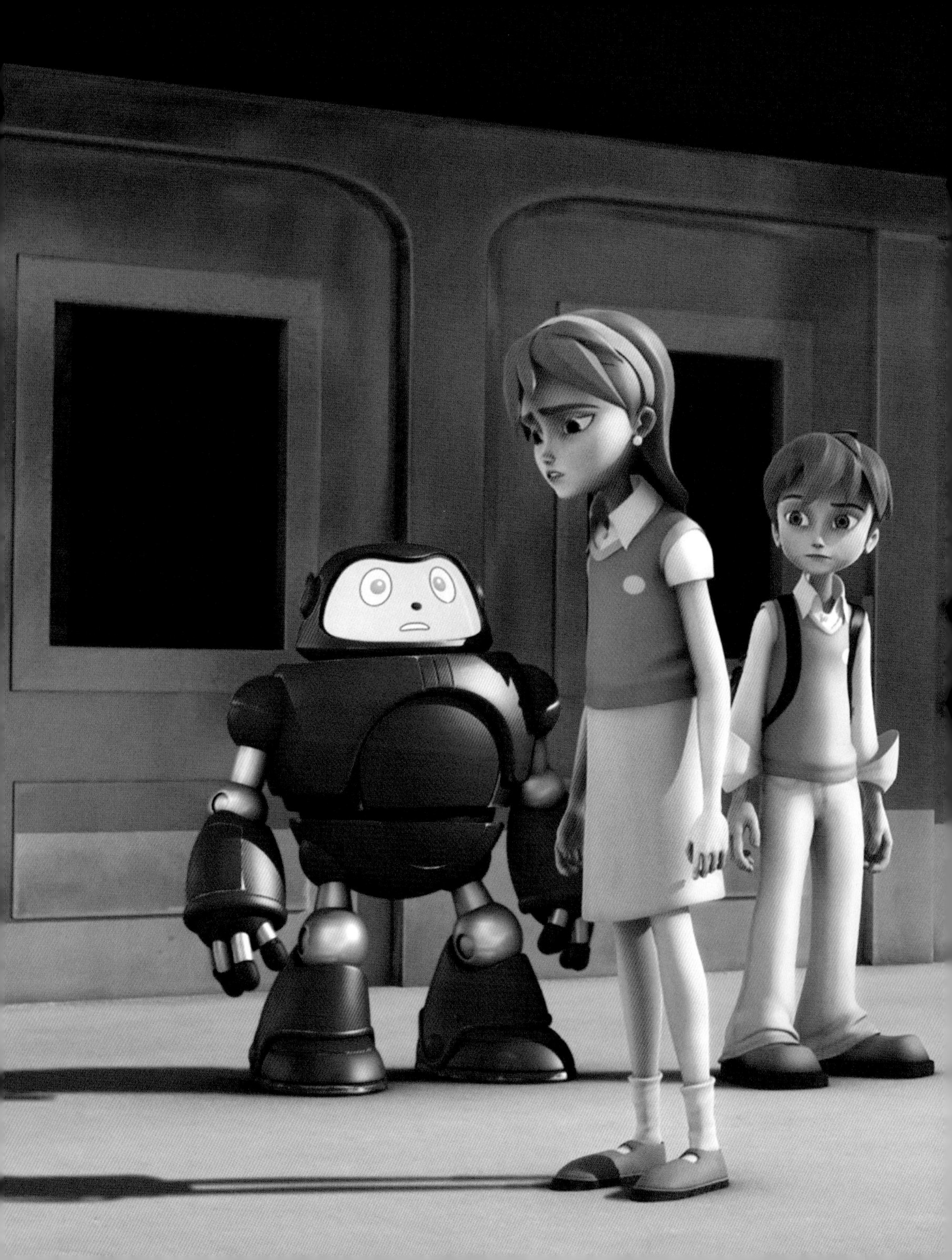

Just before the girls' club meeting, Joy talked to her friend Chris and his robot, Gizmo. She was upset that Janice didn't want someone in a wheelchair to join.

Chris said, "That's not right. You should tell her."

"No way," Joy moaned. "She's the president and could kick me out of the club. I can't stand up to Janice—I'm not that brave!"

Just then, Superbook appeared! Gizmo tried to sneak out, but Superbook quickly whisked away all three friends.

As they flew, Superbook announced, “I am taking you to meet someone who found the courage to speak up for what was right—no matter what the cost!”

Plop! They landed by a huge palace. Gizmo pulled out his scanner and reported that they were in ancient Persia, about five hundred years before Jesus was born.

They were far away from home and far back in time!

Chris looked around and whispered, “We should hide before someone sees us.”

Too late! They were spotted by the master of the palace servants. He declared, “You have been brought here to serve King Xerxes!”

He ordered Chris and Gizmo, “You two, clean all the chariots!” Next, he told a servant, “Take that girl to serve Queen Esther.” Joy looked at Chris helplessly as she was led away.

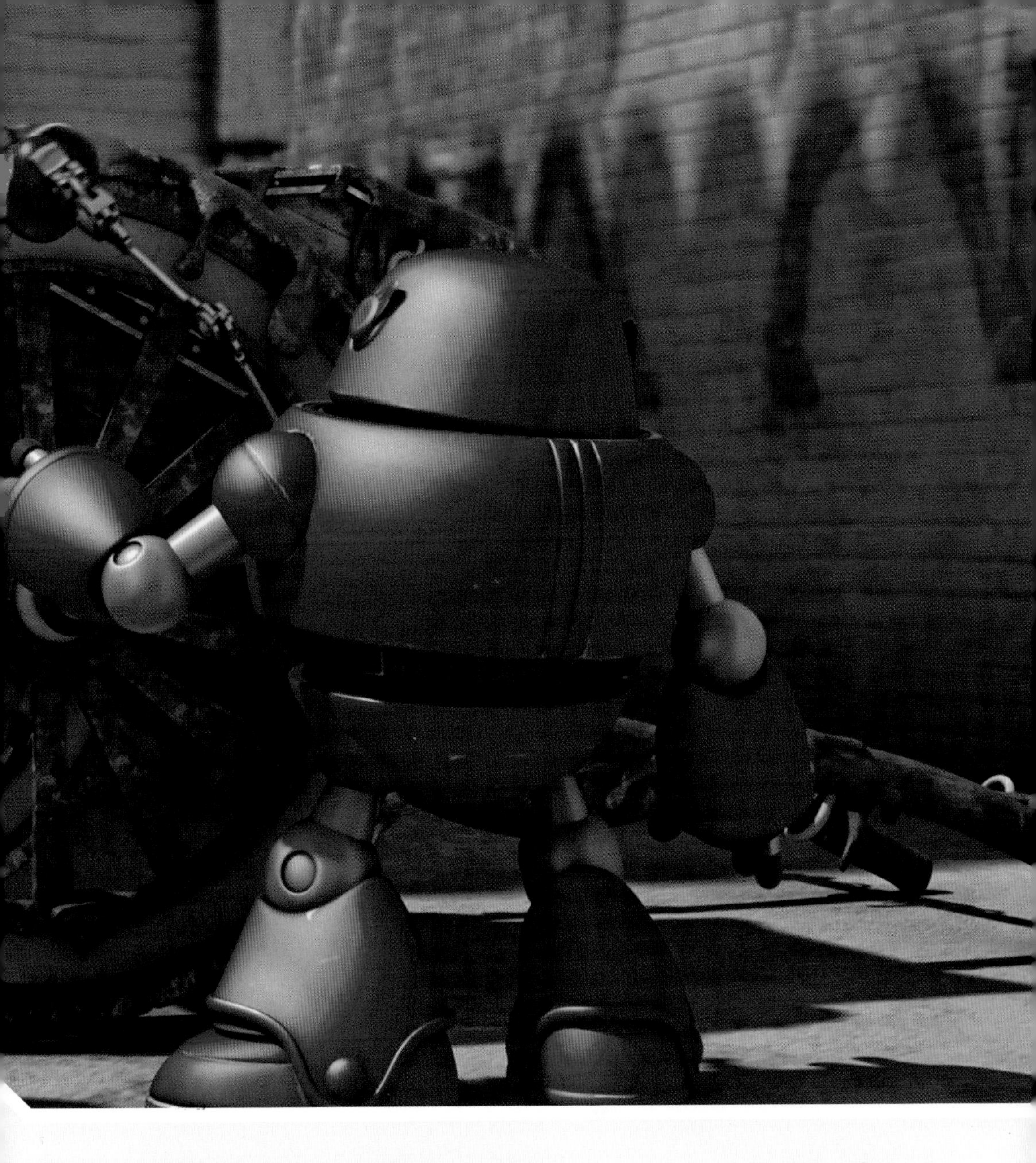

Chris stood there, wondering how to rescue Joy. But Gizmo instantly pulled out his amazing scrubber and went to work scouring mud from the chariots.

One of those chariots belonged to Haman, the king's most important official. In fact, he was so important that all the people bowed to him.

As Haman drove his chariot to the palace one day, everyone bowed down—well, everyone except a man named Mordecai. He was Jewish and only bowed to God.

Haman was angry that Mordecai would not bow to him. He decided to get rid of Mordecai, along with every other Jewish person in the empire!

So Haman told the king, “The Jews do not keep your laws. Why don’t you write a decree saying the Jews must be destroyed?”

“All right,” said the king. “Write the decree and stamp it

with my ring to make it official." Haman wrote the new law and sent messengers to announce it throughout the kingdom.

But there was something that the king did not know. His wife, Queen Esther, was Jewish!

Inside the palace, Joy was getting to know Queen Esther.

One day as they stood on the balcony, Esther pointed and said, "There is my cousin Mordecai. My parents died when I was a child, and he took very good care of me. When I grew up, he brought me here to the palace!"

"Why is he all dirty?" asked Joy.

The queen replied, "He is wearing rough sackcloth, with ashes on his head. It means he is very sad and upset about something!"

Esther quickly sent a servant to ask Mordecai what was wrong.

The servant came back and reported, “Mordecai said Haman has issued a decree to kill all the Jews. He wants you to go to the king and persuade him to stop this awful plan!”

But Esther said, “Tell Mordecai I can’t go see the king unless he asks me to come, or I could be put to death.”

Then Mordecai sent her this message: “Perhaps you were made queen for such a time as this—to save your people.”

Esther had a big decision to make. What should she do?

She told Mordecai, “Tell all the Jews to fast for me. Do not eat or drink for three days and nights. My maids and I will do the same. Although it’s against the law, I will go in to see the king.”

Then she added, “If I must die, I must die.”

A few days later Queen Esther went in to see the king.

Would he hold out his golden rod to welcome her, or would he be angry and send her away to die?

As she bowed before the king, everyone in the room held their breath. Slowly the king held out his rod to the queen. He was glad to see her! “What would you like from me, Esther?” the king asked kindly.

But Esther didn't tell him yet. She simply said, "Please come to a banquet at my palace—and bring Haman."

Haman was filled with pride to attend such a special dinner with the king and queen. And when Esther asked the two men back for a second dinner the next night, he bragged to his friends about his power.

That evening, the king asked Esther, “What do you want from me? I will give you up to half my kingdom.”

Esther boldly declared, “I want you to save me and my

people, for we are all to be killed."

The king was shocked. He exclaimed, "Who would do such a thing?"

At that, Esther pointed at Haman.

The king was furious! He rushed outside to think.

Chris and Gizmo found Joy in the palace just in time to see what would happen next!

Haman knew he was in big trouble. He started begging Esther for his life. He even grabbed the queen and held on to her! At that very moment, the king returned.

“What is this?” shouted the king. “Take him away!”

After that, Esther, Mordecai, and all of the Jews in Persia were saved!

Superbook took the children back to school as the girls' club meeting was about to begin. Chris told Joy, "Good luck!"

"I don't need luck," said Joy. "God is always with me to help me do what's right."

At the meeting Janice asked her, "Are you ready to recommend a new member?"

"Yes, I am," Joy answered confidently. "I recommend Bonnie Scott because she is smart and kind and funny."

"I think that's a bad choice," said Janice. "Let's take a vote."

At first, only Joy raised her hand. It was very quiet in the room.

Then another girl raised her hand, and another, and another—until everyone but Janice had voted yes.

Finally Janice admitted, "I guess you're right, Joy," and raised her hand too.

Together the girls went to decorate the gym. There was Gizmo, speeding around on his roller skates and launching balloons up to the ceiling.

"Nice wheels, Gizmo," said Bonnie as she zoomed around in her wheelchair to help.

"Nice wheels yourself," replied Gizmo. And the two of them shot confetti up in the air as everyone cheered.

“Who knows if perhaps you were made queen for just such a time as this?

—Esther 4:14